It's Quacking Time!

For John Joseph Harrison,
weight 7lb 11oz ∼ M.W.

For Harry James Humphreys,
my grandson ∼ J.B.

First published 2005 by Walker Books Ltd
87 Vauxhall Walk, London SE11 5HJ

10 9 8 7 6 5 4 3 2 1

Text © 2005 Martin Waddell
Illustrations © 2005 Jill Barton

The moral rights of the author and illustrator have been asserted

This book has been typeset in Esprit Medium

Printed in Singapore

British Library Cataloguing in Publication Data:
a catalogue record for this book is available from the British Library

ISBN 1-84428-009-8 (hb)
ISBN 0-7445-9861-3 (pb)

www.walkerbooks.co.uk

It's Quacking Time!

Martin Waddell

illustrated by Jill Barton

WALKER BOOKS
AND SUBSIDIARIES
LONDON • BOSTON • SYDNEY • AUCKLAND

Duckling lived in the rushes
with Mummy and Daddy.

One day Mummy Duck laid an egg.

It was pale blue.

Mummy and Daddy were excited but …

Duckling had never seen a duck egg before.
"What's that thing?" asked Duckling.

"It's our egg," Mummy said.
"Our egg with a baby duck in it."

"Did I come in one of those eggs?"
Duckling asked Daddy.

"You did," Daddy said.
"Your egg was lovely!"

Auntie Duck came up from her nest in the reeds.

"Mummy laid our egg," Duckling told Auntie.

"It's our egg with a baby duck in it. I came in one too. Daddy says my egg was lovely."

"I remember your egg," Auntie said.

"How did I fit in my egg?" Duckling asked Auntie.

"You were much smaller then," Auntie said.

"You had to be small to fit in the egg."

Granda Duck swam up from the end of the lake.

"That's our egg," Duckling told Granda. "There's a baby duck in our egg. I came in one too. Auntie says I had to be small to fit in the egg … but I don't remember my egg."

"I don't remember mine either," said Granda.

"Did you come in an egg?" Duckling gasped.

"All ducks do," Granda said.

Cousin Small Duck paddled up,
and he looked at the egg.
"What's that?" he asked Duckling.

"It's our egg, with a baby duck in it,"
Duckling said. "You came in one too."

"I didn't!" said Cousin Small.

"You did!" Duckling said.

"Granda says
all ducks do."

"Maybe Granda's wrong,"
said Cousin Small.

"Granda's *always* right,"
Duckling said. "You just
wait and see."

Mummy Duck sat on the egg.

Daddy Duck came with some food.

"Our egg moved a bit," Duckling told Daddy.

Auntie Duck came with some
feathers to make the nest cosy and nice.
"Our egg jiggled a bit," Duckling told Auntie.

Granda Duck came to see
how things were going.

"I heard something inside our egg,"
Duckling told Granda.

Mummy Duck stood up.

"It won't be long now," she told Duckling.

All the big ducks were excited.

They stood round the egg and they quacked.

Quack-quack-quack-quack!

But ...

nothing happened.

Then Duckling quacked at the egg,
all by himself, very softly.
"Quack-quack-quack!"
and ...

tap-
tap-
tap!

"Our egg tapped at me!"
Duckling gasped.

Then ...
crack!
The egg broke.

And out of the shell poked a tiny wee beak,
and a tiny wee head, just like Duckling's,
but very much smaller.

"Oh my goodness!"
gasped Cousin Small.

It was quacking time
at the lake.

Quack!

Quack!
Quack!

And they all loved
their new baby duck.

The End